An I Can Read Book™

Emma's STRANGE PET

story by **Jean Little**

pictures by **Jennifer Plecas**

HarperCollins*Publishers*

HarperCollins®, ✚®, and I Can Read Book® are
trademarks of HarperCollins Publishers Inc.

Emma's Strange Pet
Text copyright © 2003 by Jean Little
Illustrations copyright © 2003 by Jennifer Plecas
Printed in the U.S.A. All rights reserved
www.harperchildrens.com

Library of Congress Cataloging-in-Publication Data
Little, Jean, 1932–
Emma's strange pet / story by Jean Little ; pictures by Jennifer Plecas.
   p.   cm. — (An I can read book)
Summary: Emma is allergic to animals with fur, but because she and her adopted brother
really want a pet, they decide to try a lizard.
   ISBN 0-06-028350-5 — ISBN 0-06-028351-3 (lib. bdg.) — ISBN 0-06-444259-4 (pbk.)
   [1. Lizards as pets—Fiction.   2. Pets—Fiction   3. Brothers and sisters—Fiction.
4. Allergy—Fiction.   5. Adoption—Fiction.]   I. Plecas, Jennifer, ill.   II. Title.   III. Series.
PZ7.L7225 En   2002   2001016637
[E]—dc21

❖

CONTENTS

Pet Wanted

Max was playing

with Josh and Sally's dog, Lucky.

"Fetch the ball, Lucky," Max called.

Lucky took the ball to Josh.

"He always does that," Josh said.

"He knows he's my dog."

"I'm going to get a dog," Max said.

"My new dad will get me one.

My dog will be better than Lucky."

Sally looked up from her book.

"No, Max," she called down.

"Dogs make Emma sneeze.

They won't get you one."

"That's not true!" Max shouted.

"I will so get a dog!"

He ran home.

Dad was starting to cook.

"Time to eat, Max," he said.

Max sat across from Emma.

"I want a dog," he said,

"a dog like Lucky, only all mine.

Sally says I can't have one.

That's not true, is it?"

Emma put down her hot dog.

"I'm sorry, Max," Dad said.

"Sally is right.

We can't get you a dog.

Emma is allergic to them.

They make her sneeze and wheeze,

and they make her eyes sore."

"I don't want a dog for Emma.

I want a dog for me," Max said.

"I know it is hard, Max," Mom said.

"It is hard for Emma, too,

but we can't have furry pets."

Emma said nothing.

Max did not give up.

"How about a cat?" he asked.

"No cats," said Mom.

"A rabbit?" Max tried.

"No rabbits, Max," said Dad.

"We can't have any pet with fur."

Max jumped up.

His face got very red.

"That's not fair!" he yelled.

"All good pets have fur.

Only strange pets have no fur.

I want a furry pet like Lucky!"

14

Then Emma surprised her family.

"I want a pet, too," she said.

"My birthday is next Saturday.

I want a pet for my birthday,

and a strange pet will be just fine."

Mr. Brown's Pet Store

Emma's birthday came at last.

Max and Emma ate fast.

"Let's go to the pet store!" Max said.

"Right now?" asked Mom.

"Yes, yes, YES!" shouted Max.

"Please, Mom," said Emma.

"Just let me drink my tea," Mom said.

Dad and Mom walked to the car.

Emma and Max ran.

They drove to Mr. Brown's Pet Store.

At the store,

Max ran to look at everything.

Emma went around slowly.

Mr. Brown had birds and fish.

He had mice and hamsters.

And he had one small lizard.

Emma stopped to look at it.

"That's an anole," said Mr. Brown.

"Did you say 'a hole'?" Emma asked.

"No." Mr. Brown smiled. "An anole."

The tiny anole looked up at Emma.

"He looks sad," Emma said.

"I had two of them," said Mr. Brown.

"Today I sold the other one.

Maybe he misses his friend."

"How about a bird,
Emma?" Dad said.

"Or a beautiful fish?"
asked Mom.

"Here's a great rat!"
said Max.

21

"I want this lizard," Emma said.

Max ran to see.

"Hi, strange pet," he said.

"He's an anole," Emma said.

Max jumped up and down.

"Emma, name him Stranger," he said.

"Good thinking, Max," said Emma.

"Stranger is just right for him."

She smiled at her new pet.

"Hi, Stranger," she said softly.

Mr. Brown put Stranger in a box.

"He likes live food," said Mr. Brown.

"Feed him crickets and meal worms."

Mom made a face.

"I will feed Stranger," Emma said.

"He changes color," said Mr. Brown.

"He can go from brown to green
and from green to brown."

"Can he turn red?" asked Max.

"No, Max," Mr. Brown said.

"Just brown and green."

Dad got a fish tank and food.

Emma picked up Stranger's box.

"Let's go home, boy," she said.

A Place for Stranger

In the car,

Max looked at Stranger's box.

"I still like furry pets," he said.

At home, Emma put sand in the tank.

Max found flat rocks outside.

Dad found a piece of wood
with a hole in it.
"Lizards like to hide," he said.
"Stranger can hide behind this.
He can peek out of the hole."
Mom got a flat water dish.

Emma put Stranger on the sand.

He stayed still for ages.

Emma and Max watched.

Slowly, the green anole grew brown.

Soon he looked like the sand.

Then Stranger saw the wood.

He shot across the tank

and hid behind it.

Then he peeked out.

"He thinks we can't see him.

He's sweet," Emma said softly.

"I guess so," said Max,

"but he sure is a strange pet."

Max reached in to poke Stranger.

"Don't, Max," Emma told him.

"Stranger is not a pet to play with.

He is a pet to watch.

Let's feed him."

"Yes, yes, YES!" shouted Max.

Emma got tweezers.

She caught a cricket

and held it near Stranger.

It wiggled.

Stranger's head shot around.

SNAP!

Stranger snapped up the cricket.

A leg hung out of his mouth.

Then the leg was gone, too.

"Wow," Max said.

"Your turn, Max," said Emma.

Adopting Stranger

Stranger snapped up crickets.

He drank water from his dish.

He sat still a lot.

Emma loved him.

She fed him and talked to him.

"He isn't sad now," she told Sally.

"He's still strange," Max said.

But Max got Josh to come over.

Josh watched Stranger eat.

The anole turned from green to brown.

"Put him on my shirt," Josh said.

"Maybe he will go red all over."

"No way," Emma said.

"He won't go red all over,

and it might hurt him."

"No way," said Max.

"Be nice to Stranger.

He is like me, you know."

Emma stared at her brother.

"How?" she asked.

"You adopted me," said Max,

"and you sort of adopted him.

He was a stranger, like me.

Then he came here, like me.

He has a new home.

He has a new family.

Just like me.

Now we both belong here."

Emma thought about it.

"You are right," Emma said at last.

"But I'm glad you are not an anole.

I would not want a green brother."

"Open up, Max," said Josh.

"Eat your nice meal worm."

Even Max had to laugh.

Where Is Stranger?

One day,

Emma went to look at Stranger.

He was not on the rocks.

He was not behind the wood.

Stranger was gone.

Emma ran to Max's room.

"Where is he?" she asked.

Max did not look at Emma.

"Where's who?" he said.

Max's face was red.

Emma was sure he knew

where her pet was.

"Tell me right now!" she shouted.

"Tell me, or I'm telling Mom!"

"Don't," Max said.

"Stranger is okay.

He's just hiding, Emma.

Try to find him."

Emma wanted to hit Max.

But he was only four.

She looked around.

Stranger wasn't on the table.

He wasn't on the bed.

Emma did not see her pet.

She couldn't stand it.

She grabbed Max.

"Where is he, Max?"

she shouted.

Then Emma saw her pet.

Stranger was peeping out at her.

He was on top of Max's head,

hiding in Max's hair.

Emma had to laugh.

She picked Stranger up.

"You love him, too," she said.

"I like furry pets better," Max said,

"but I wish Stranger was mine."

"I like furry pets, too," said Emma,

"but lizards are great."

"My birthday is far away,"

Max said sadly.

"When it comes, I want one."

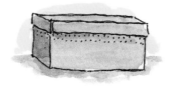

A Friend for Stranger

Emma put Stranger back in his tank.

Then she called Dad.

She told him about Max.

"Stranger needs a friend," she said,

"and Max's birthday is too far away."

"Max is only four," Dad said.

"Max is good with Stranger,"

Emma said. "I know

he can do it, Dad."

Dad came home with a box.

"What's that?" Max asked.

"Look and see," said Dad.

In the box there was another anole.

"Is he for Emma?" Max asked.

"This one is for you," Dad said.

"Emma says he can live with Stranger.

How about it, Max?

Do you want a strange pet?"

"Yes, yes, YES!" shouted Max.

"He will be my very own.

I will adopt you, Wizard."

"Is his name Wizard?" Emma asked.

"Wizard the Lizard," said Max.

"He can turn from green to brown.

That takes a wizard."

Max ran to Stranger's tank
and put Wizard down on a rock.
Everyone watched.

Stranger shot behind the wood.

He peeked out at Wizard.

Wizard hid behind the rocks.

"I hope they get along," said Dad.

"They will," said Emma.

"Yes," said Max. "They will.

Look at me and Emma.

She is strange,

but we get along just fine."

E
LIT

Little, Jean.

Emma's strange pet.

J

$16.89

DATE			